Dedicated to my son.

This  gab Book belongs to

_____

THE
PAPER
CROWN

WRITTEN BY
Andrew Torba
ILLUSTRATION BY DISCO

Once upon a time, in a tiny village, there lived a little boy named Samuel.

In this lovely village where he lived, his father had a special way of helping his son's imagination grow.

From a very young age, Samuel's father would tell him stories about kings and heroes, tales of bravery and leadership.

He would talk about famous rulers
who had shaped history, their
names remembered for all time.

Samuel would listen, his eyes
wide with wonder, as his father
painted pictures of big kingdoms
and exciting battles.

His father often ended these stories by saying to Samuel, "You, my son, are a hero in the making. Just like those great leaders, you too have the power to make a difference in the world."

"Your job is to lead, to inspire,
and to build a legacy that will
last forever, not just for now,
but in Heaven, too."

7

These words put a dream in Samuel's heart, a wish to one day become a leader. So he fashioned a crown out of some newspaper and put it on his head.

Then he built a castle out of the couch cushions.

9

He imagined ruling over a
happy land and making things
better for everyone.

10

He dreamed about living in a real castle and of defeating dragons. He wanted to be a king.

One day, he told his father about
this plan to become a king.

His father, a wise and gentle man, asked Samuel a question. "My son, do you know what makes a good king?" Samuel realized that he didn't know the answer.

So his father asked Samuel to sit down and began to teach him about the Christian duties of a king.

"A good king," his father explained,
"must be fair and just. He must always
be caring and kind to his people."

"He must be humble, putting the needs of his people before his own wishes."

"A true king must also be brave,
standing up for what is right.
He must always protect the
ones who need help."

His father continued, "He doesn't always wear a gold crown, but he must always wear a crown of righteousness."

18

Samuel listened carefully to
his father's words.

19

He started to see that being a king was not just about wearing a golden crown and having a castle.

It was also about serving others and living according to Christian principles.

21

Samuel turned to his father and said, "Dad, being a king sounds a lot like you are. You are always kind and fair, and you work hard to help our village."

22

He took off his paper crown.
"Instead of being a king, I think
I want to be like you."

His father smiled warmly at Samuel and hugged him.

"My son, you have learned a very important lesson today. Being a good leader is not about the title or the crown, but about the way you live your life and treat others."

"If you follow the teachings of
Jesus and obey God's Word, you
will make a difference in the world,
no matter what your job may be."

From that day on, Samuel focused on being a good Christian man of great character, just like his father.

He grew up to be a wise and caring man, loved and respected by everyone who knew him.

28

And although he never became a king, Samuel knew that he had found something more valuable.

29

He had found the joy of helping
others and living a life guided by
his faith, just like his father.

The end.

Being a king isn't always about wearing a crown of gold. It's about wearing a crown of righteousness and taking on the responsibilities and duties of being a leader. As Christians we look to the King of kings and Lord of lords, Jesus Christ, for the ultimate example of kingship in our lives.

Christ is King

About the author:

Andrew Torba is a Christian entrepreneur and best selling author from rural Pennsylvania. He and his wife Emily have three children.

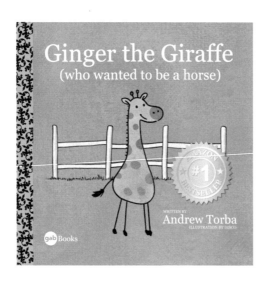

Made in United States
Troutdale, OR
11/21/2024